Me and Ms. Too

By **Laura Ruby**

Illustrated by **Dung Ho**

BALZER + BRAY
An Imprint of HarperCollins Publishers

For Melissa and Jessica, who forgave me
when I didn't know how to cut the kiwis—L.R.

For Tung, my partner in crime—D.H.

Balzer + Bray is an imprint of HarperCollins Publishers.

Me and Ms. Too
Text copyright © 2022 by Laura Ruby
Illustrations copyright © 2022 by Thi Hanh Dung Ho

ISBN 978-0-06-289433-5

The artist used Adobe Photoshop to create the digital illustrations for this book.
Typography by Chelsea C. Donaldson
21 22 23 24 25 RTLO 10 9 8 7 6 5 4 3 2 1
❖
First Edition

When Dad married Ms. Too,
everything changed.

Even the wallpaper.

I liked that wallpaper.

"But Molly, you said it looked like a bunch of angry thumbs," Dad said.

"That was before."

"Before what?"

Before Ms. Too, my house looked like my house and nobody else's. My dad was my dad and nobody else's.

Ms. Too said, "That wallpaper was a little loud."
"Wallpaper isn't loud," I said. "People are loud."
"Sometimes," said Ms. Too.

After school, Ms. Too picked me up and watched me till
dinner. She took me to the pool and the park and the zoo.
I liked the pool and the park and the zoo.

But I didn't like Ms. Too.

"But Molly, I thought she was your favorite," Dad said.

That was before.

"Before what?"

Before, Dad took me to the pool and the park and the zoo.

We splashed

and we spun

and we laughed
at the llamas.

When we got home, we cooked breakfast for dinner and dinner for breakfast. We baked cookies shaped like funny little bunnies.

And we sang all day long.

Ms. Too didn't like to do any of those things.
She took me to the pool, but she didn't like to splash.

She took me to the park,
but she didn't like to spin.

She liked cats better than people.

She couldn't make meatballs or muffins or funny little bunnies.

She didn't cut the kiwis right.

And her books took up all the room in the house.

"But Molly, I thought you loved books," Dad said.

That was before.

Before, Ms. Too was just plain old Ms. Blue, the librarian. She read us stories. She helped me find just the right books.

Until one day, Dad heard her read a story out loud. His eyes got all watery, like he wanted to cry. Then he put his hand on his heart.

I thought I was his heart.

The wedding was in our backyard,
right by my sandbox.

I said Ms. Too's dress looked like underwear.
I said my stomach hurt.
I said we were just a bunch of funny little bunnies.
"Maybe we are a funny kind of family, but I like
that about us," said Dad.

I didn't like it.

Every time we went somewhere, I asked: "Is *she* coming too?"

"*Ms. Blue, Ms. Blue, now you are a Too, Ms. Too,*" my dad sang.

But Ms. Too didn't mind her new nickname.

And she didn't mind taking me places after school,
even if she didn't like them so much herself.

"Let's go see the cats," she said.

"Cats are scratchy," I said.

"Sometimes. Look!"

Inside an enclosure were a big cat and a little one. The zookeeper explained that the big cat was once cranky and lonely, and a stray kitten moved in to keep it company. They did everything together. We watched them for a long while.

They ate their kibble side by side.

They batted a ball back and forth.

They curled in the sun and fell asleep.

My stomach felt funny.
"There are all kinds of families,"
said Ms. Too.

When we got home, Ms. Too pulled a book off the shelf and found a recipe for cookies. She kept looking at the ingredients and then at the instructions. She seemed cranky.

I said, "Do you want me to help you?"

"I was hoping you would ask," she said. "Thank you."

Together, we read the instructions. Together, we mixed the dough. Together, we made cookies in the shape of underwear, of a bunch of angry thumbs, of big cats and little ones.

We had a blob of dough left over. She shaped it with her hands.

After it was baked, she put it on a plate and gave it to me. "You will always be your daddy's heart, you know. And mine, too."

Now when we go to the pool and the park and the zoo,

we dive

and we swing

and we purr at the cats.

We make cookies in the shape of everything we see and anything we wish. We meow as we cook. Sometimes we are loud.

And she still reads me the best stories. Maybe we are a funny kind of family.

But I like that about us.